PUMPKIN ORANGE, PUMPKIN ROUND

by Rosanna Battigelli   Illustrated by Tara Anderson

pajamapress

Pumpkin orange,
pumpkin round,

pumpkin hiding...
pumpkin found!

Pumpkin lifting,
pumpkin fall,

pumpkin rolling,
pumpkin ball!

Pumpkin partridge,
pumpkin mouse,
pumpkin wheeling,
pumpkin house.

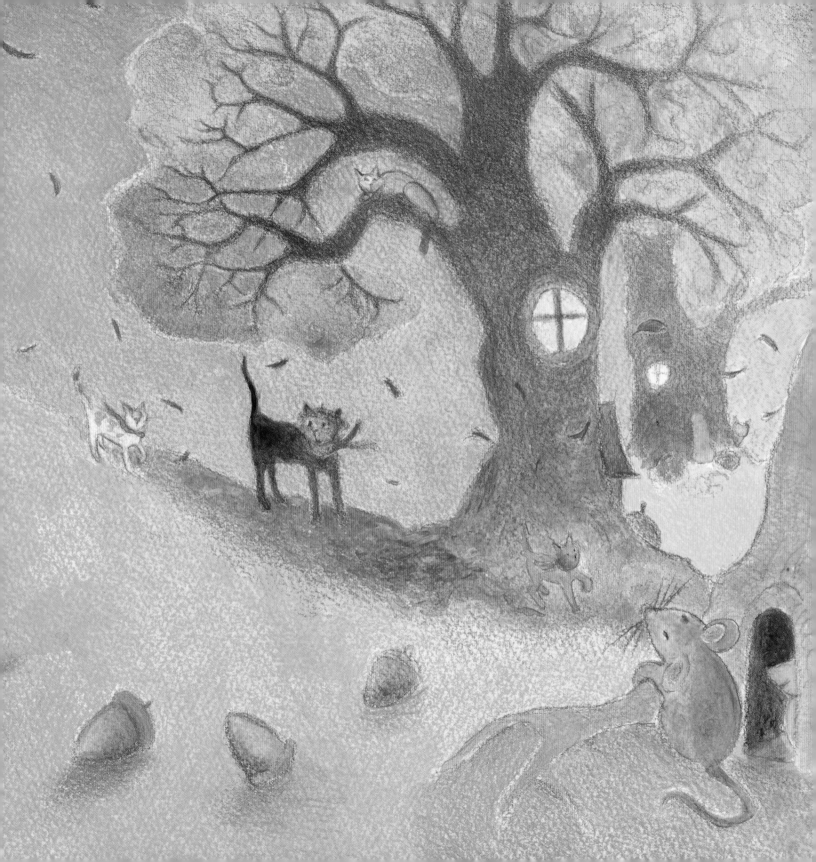

Pumpkin seedy,
pumpkin slime,
pumpkin empty,
pumpkin mine!

Pumpkin drawing,
pumpkin trace,
pumpkin carving,
pumpkin face!

Pumpkin gleaming,
pumpkin glow,
pumpkin glaring,
pumpkin show!

Pumpkin pirate,
pumpkin prance,
pumpkin fairy,
pumpkin dance!

Pumpkin flashlight,
pumpkin chum,
pumpkin neighbor,
pumpkin mom.

Pumpkin mask,
pumpkin dare,

pumpkin candy,
pumpkin scare!

Pumpkin lantern,
pumpkin light,

pumpkin children,
pumpkin night.

Pumpkin tired,
pumpkin fed,
    pumpkin story,
    pumpkin bed.

First published in Canada and the United States in 2019

Text copyright © 2019 Rosanna Battigelli
Illustration copyright © 2019 Tara Anderson
This edition copyright © 2019 Pajama Press Inc.
This is a first edition.

10 9 8 7 6 5 4 3 2 1

Canada Council   Conseil des arts
for the Arts   du Canada

ONTARIO ARTS COUNCIL
CONSEIL DES ARTS DE L'ONTARIO
an Ontario government agency
un organisme du gouvernement de l'Ontario

Canadä

The publisher gratefully acknowledges the support of the Canada Council for the Arts and the Ontario Arts Council for its
publishing program. We acknowledge the financial support of the Government of Canada through the Canada Book Fund
(CBF) for our publishing activities.

Library and Archives Canada Cataloguing in Publication

Title: Pumpkin orange, pumpkin round / by Rosanna Battigelli ; illustrated by Tara Anderson.
Names: Battigelli, Rosanna, author. | Anderson, Tara, illustrator.
Identifiers: Canadiana 20190088451 | ISBN 9781772780925 (hardcover)
Classification: LCC PS8553.A83 P86 2019 | DDC jC813/.54—dc23

Publisher Cataloging-in-Publication Data (U.S.)

Names: Battigelli, Rosanna, author. | Anderson, Tara, illustrator.
Title: Pumpkin Orange, Pumpkin Round / by Rosanna Battigelli; illustrated by Tara Anderson.
Description: Toronto, Ontario Canada : Pajama Press, 2019. | Summary: "Short, rhyming lines take a family of cats through
each step of carving jack-o-lanterns: visiting the pumpkin patch and taking home their selections; cleaning out the seeds
and slime; drawing designs; carving; and lighting their completed lanterns. After a fun evening of trick-or-treating at the
neighbors' houses, it's home to bed"– Provided by publisher. Identifiers: ISBN 978-1-77278-092-5 (hardcover)
Subjects: LCSH: Halloween – Juvenile fiction. |Cats – Juvenile fiction. | Jack-o-lanterns – Juvenile fiction. | Humorous
stories. | BISAC: JUVENILE FICTION / Holidays & Celebrations / Halloween. | JUVENILE FICTION / Stories in Verse.
Classification: LCC PZ7.B388Pum |DDC [E] – dc23

Original art created
with colored pencil and acrylic
glaze on watercolor paper

Cover and book design–Rebecca Bender

Manufactured by Qualibre Inc./Printplus
Printed in China

Pajama Press Inc.
181 Carlaw Ave. Suite 251 Toronto, Ontario Canada, M4M 2S1

Distributed in Canada by UTP Distribution
5201 Dufferin Street Toronto, Ontario Canada, M3H 5T8

Distributed in the U.S. by Ingram Publisher Services
1 Ingram Blvd. La Vergne, TN 37086, USA

For my darling little pumpkin,
Rosalie Cara, whose light
shines right into my heart
-R.B.

Pumpkin friends for Alice,
Lilly, Dean, Colin, Toby,
and baby Elliot
-T.A.

You Can Carve a

YOU WILL NEED:

A pumpkin
An adult helper
A child-safe pumpkin carving kit
A marker
A battery-powered candle
Clothes that can get messy

HOW TO:

1. Have your adult helper carefully cut a large hole in the top of the pumpkin, angling the sides inward so that the "lid" will not fall into the hole.
2. Using a scoop or your hands, remove all the seeds and slime from the pumpkin.
3. Using a marker, draw a face on the front of the pumpkin. Remember to use closed shapes instead of lines.
4. Have your adult helper carefully cut out your shapes.
5. Reach through the big hole to place a battery-powered candle inside the pumpkin and place the "lid" over the hole.
6. Enjoy your glowing jack-o-lantern.